To Evangeline

Happy Christmas 1999.

Lots of love from

Mummy + Daddy

xxx

A catalogue record for this book is available
from the British Library

Published by Ladybird Books Ltd
A subsidiary of the Penguin Group
A Pearson Company

LADYBIRD and the device of a Ladybird are trademarks of
Ladybird Books Ltd Loughborough Leicestershire UK

© Disney MCMXCVII

Adapted from Walt Disney Pictures' **Hercules**

Music by Alan Menken   Lyrics by David Zippel   Original score by Alan Menken
Produced by Alice Dewey and John Musker & Ron Clements
Directed by John Musker & Ron Clements

DISNEY'S
HERCULES

Ladybird

Long ago, powerful gods lived on Mount Olympus in ancient Greece, ruled by the mighty god Zeus.

One day, there was a great celebration. Zeus and his wife, Hera, had a baby boy. "I shall name him Hercules," said Zeus. "He will be the strongest god of all." Everyone brought gifts to honour baby Hercules. The finest was a winged horse called Pegasus from Zeus and Hera.

However, one god didn't share in the joy of the day. This was Hades, god of the Underworld – a dark, gloomy place where spirits of the dead were sent.

Hades was jealous of Zeus – *he* wanted to rule Olympus. Hades consulted the Fates – three old women who could see the past, present and future with the one eye they shared. "In eighteen years," the Fates told Hades, "the time will be right to release the Titans and conquer Olympus. However," they continued, "if Hercules fights for the gods, your plan will fail." Hades was determined – Hercules would not stand in his way.

So, one dark night, Hades sent his
assistants, Pain and Panic, to kidnap the
baby. They took Hercules to Earth and
fed him a potion to make him mortal, so
they could get rid of him for good.

Luckily, just before Hercules could drink
the very last drop, a couple interrupted
the villains' evil deed. Pain and Panic fled
back to the Underworld. Hercules, who
was now mortal, was left behind.

The couple, Amphitryon and Alcmene, had always longed for a child of their own and decided to take care of Hercules themselves.

Meanwhile, Hades, believing that Hercules was no longer a problem, looked forward to his conquest of Olympus.

Hercules grew up to be a fine young man. As he hadn't finished all of Hades' potion, he kept his godlike strength. But this strength often got him into trouble – even when he was only trying to help! Soon, Hercules was shunned by all the townsfolk. His earthly parents decided it was time to tell him the truth. They showed Hercules the medallion he was wearing when they found him. It had the symbol of the gods on it.

"Perhaps the gods can help me," said Hercules. He went to the temple of the god Zeus and prayed.

Suddenly, the enormous statue of Zeus came to life. "I am your real father," he said. Hercules was amazed.

"If Olympus is my home, let me come back there with you!" Hercules cried.

"Only gods can live on Olympus," said Zeus, sadly. "You will have to prove yourself a true hero on Earth before you can return."

Zeus told Hercules to seek the help of Philoctetes – trainer of heroes. Then he reunited his son with the winged horse, Pegasus.

Hercules and Pegasus set out in search of the famous trainer, Phil, who was half goat, half man. When they tracked him down, Hercules explained that he needed his help.

"I'm retired," said Phil, walking off.

Zeus, who was keeping an *eye* on his son, threw a lightning bolt at Phil. The little goat man quickly changed his mind – Hercules was delighted.

As time passed, Hercules slowly mastered all the hero's skills Phil could teach. One day, Hercules said to Phil, "I'm ready. I want to battle some monsters, rescue damsels – you know, heroic stuff."

"Okay," Phil agreed. "I'll take you to the city of Thebes – it's got earthquakes, fires, floods and monsters – the perfect place for a would-be hero!" And together they set off on Pegasus.

As Pegasus soared above the clouds, they heard a scream from the forest below. Megara, a beautiful young woman, was in the clutches of a centaur called Nessus. Hercules leapt into action but Meg turned down his offer of help.

However, Hercules was determined – he fought with the centaur and won.

Meg wasn't impressed. After finding out the young man's name, she left.

As Hercules, Phil and Pegasus set off for Thebes once more, Meg walked through the forest and met Hades. Meg's spirit belonged to Hades and she was forced to do his bidding.

When she said she had been saved from Nessus by Hercules, Hades flew into a rage. He resolved to destroy Hercules once and for all.

Meanwhile, Hercules had reached the great city of Thebes. He was desperate to prove to the Thebans that he could help them and was soon called upon to fight the Hydra – a vicious, evil monster.

Hercules cut off the Hydra's head but more heads appeared in its place. This continued until Hercules was battling with thirty snarling, writhing heads.

By using all the skills Phil had taught him, Hercules eventually defeated the creature. The citizens of Thebes were overjoyed.

From then on, Hercules protected the city against many more terrible monsters. Soon, he was the most popular hero around.

Little did Hercules know that all the monsters had been sent by Hades to destroy him. Hades' time was now running out. Eighteen years had passed and it was time for him to launch his attack on Olympus.

Hades knew that to get rid of Hercules, he had to discover the hero's weakness. He turned to Meg and said, "If you can give me the key to Wonder Boy, I'll give you your freedom." Meg hesitated – she knew Hercules didn't deserve this but she longed to be free.

The next day, Meg visited Hercules and they talked and laughed together. That night she told Hades she didn't want to help destroy Hercules and that the hero had no weaknesses. Suddenly, Hades realised what Hercules' one true weakness was – it was Meg!

That same night, as Hercules was training, Hades paid him a visit. He brought Meg with him. "If you give up your godlike powers for twenty-four hours," he said. "I will free her."

"Only if you swear Meg will be safe from harm," said Hercules.

Hades promised that if Meg was harmed, Hercules would get his strength back.

In a flash, Hercules lost his strength and became a true human. Then Hades announced that Meg had been working for him all the time. Meg apologised but Hercules was hurt by her betrayal.

Hades quickly unleashed the Tornado, Rock, Ice and Lava Titans—evil monsters that had incredible powers. Zeus had imprisoned the Titans many years before and now they wanted their revenge.

Hades and the powerful Titans attacked Olympus. The gods fought bravely but, despite their powers, were easily overcome. Finally, Zeus himself was captured – it seemed Hades had won.

Back in Thebes, a giant Cyclops was on the rampage. Even though he knew it was hopeless, Hercules summoned up all his courage and prepared to do battle.

But without his godlike strength, Hercules was no match for the one-eyed monster and was soon overpowered.

Meanwhile, Meg had found Phil and Pegasus. All three rushed to Hercules' aid.

"Don't give up!" cried Phil. "Not now!" But Hercules, still upset by Meg's betrayal, felt defeated. "Come on kid," whispered Phil. "I'm not going to quit on you. You can do it!"

With renewed hope, Hercules attacked the Cyclops with a burning stick. As it fell to the ground, the monster knocked over some columns. Meg saw one tumble towards Hercules and pushed him out of the way.

Hercules was saved but Meg was injured. Suddenly, Hercules' strength returned. Because Meg had been hurt, the pact with Hades was broken.

Hercules cradled Meg in his arms and asked why she had saved him. "People do crazy things when they're in love," she answered, weakly. "Now go and stop Hades."

Hercules and Pegasus soared towards Olympus and freed the gods. Together, Hercules and the gods fought the Titans. It was a colossal battle, but in the end, Mount Olympus was saved. Hercules sent the Titans spinning into the depths of space where they would remain forever.

As a defeated Hades retreated to the Underworld, he yelled smugly to Hercules, "I have a friend of yours who's *dying* to see me!"

Fear gripped Hercules. "Meg!" he cried.

Hercules rushed back to Thebes but it was too late – Meg had died. Immediately, Hercules entered the Underworld and offered his life to Hades in place of Meg's.

Hades agreed and Hercules entered the Pit of Death. This act of sacrifice made him a true hero and he became a god. Now immortal, he rescued Meg's spirit.

Realising that he was beaten, Hades begged for mercy. But, in a rage, Hercules cast him into the Pit of Death, where he would remain for all time.

Back in Thebes, Hercules reunited Meg's spirit with her body and she slowly came back to life. Then she and Hercules were lifted skyward.

At the gates of Mount Olympus stood Zeus and Hera, who proudly greeted their son. "A true hero is measured by the strength of his heart," Zeus told Hercules. "Now, at last, you can come home."

As Hercules began to walk into Olympus, he glanced back at Meg. "Father," he said to Zeus, "this is the moment I've always dreamed of, but a life without Meg is an empty one. I wish to stay on Earth with her. I finally know where I belong."

Zeus and Hera understood. They waved goodbye as Hercules, Meg and Phil flew back to Thebes on Pegasus.

That night, Zeus created a special set of stars in the shape of his son. They would shine in Hercules' honour forever.